About the Author

Born in North Yorkshire, I served a five year engineering apprenticeship and after gaining the appropriate qualifications spent many years teaching engineering. I have worked for a number of colleges as a lecturer and many industrial companies as an engineer. I live in West Yorkshire with my wife, Joan, a pharmacist. We have three married children and six grandchildren who all live in the area.

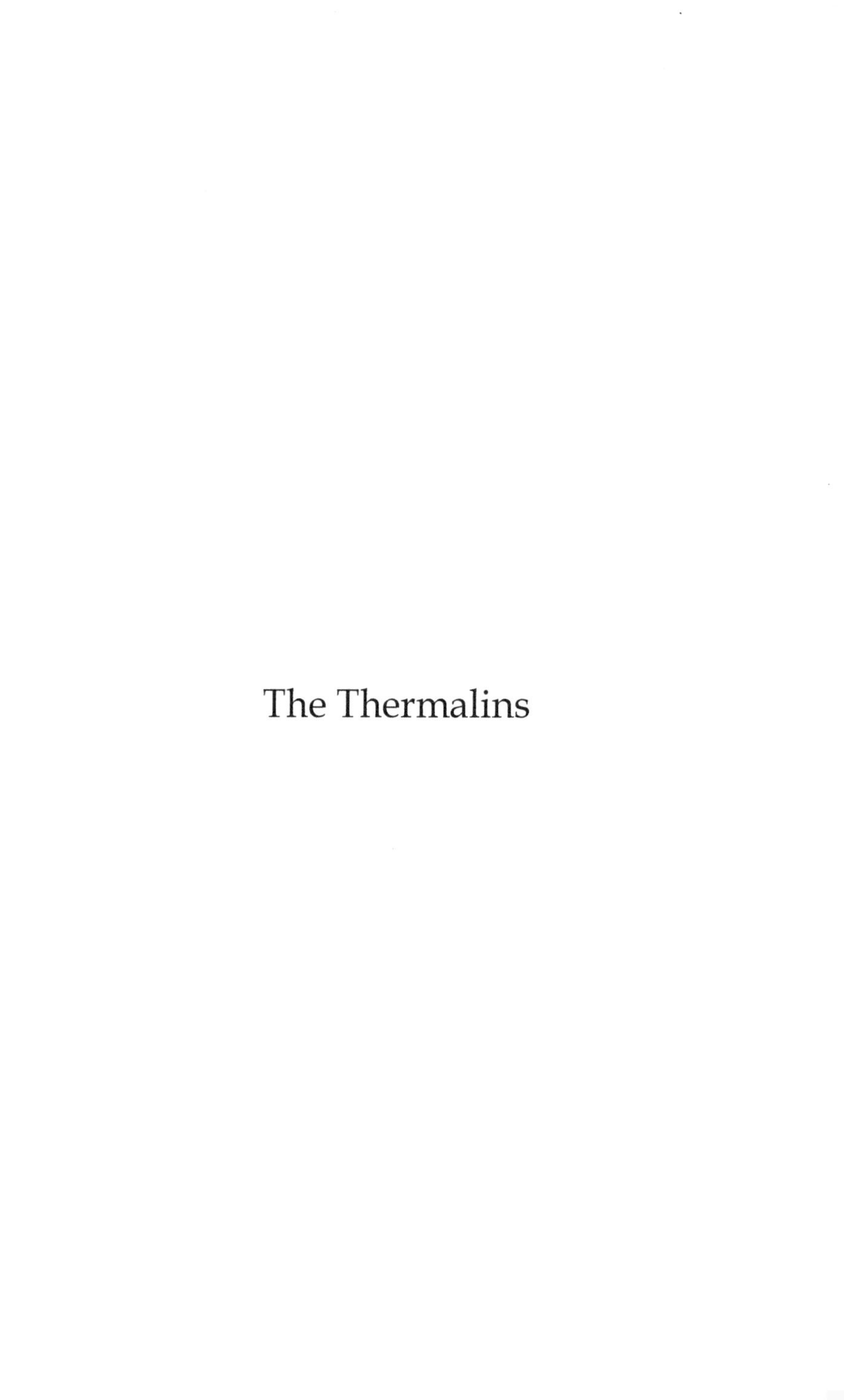

The Thermalins

Brian E Turner
Illustrations by Cathy Suzuki

The Thermalins

Nightingale Books

NIGHTINGALE PAPERBACK

A CIP catalogue record for this title is available from the British Library.
ISBN 978-1-83875-404-4

Nightingale Books is an imprint of Pegasus Elliot MacKenzie Publishers Ltd.
www.pegasuspublishers.com

First Published in 2022

Nightingale Books
Sheraton House Castle Park
Cambridge England

Printed & Bound in Great Britain

Dedication

I would like to thank my daughter, Susan, and her daughters, Jessica, Rebecca and Molly for encouraging me to have *The Thermalins* published. Thank you to my wife, Joan, for her patience as I spend time writing. A special thanks to young Molly who read my early manuscript and said her friends would love to read it.

Chapter 1
The Little People of the Woods

Long before people lived in the land, an ancient little people called the Thermalins lived in little villages deep in the woods, each of their houses were built into small mounds in the ground and cannot be seen by people. They still live in many areas in the British countryside today and can make themselves invisible to people although they sometimes can be seen by children.

The Thermalins are no more than fifteen centimetres or six inches tall when fully grown, their children are therefore smaller depending on their age.

They are very much like humans although they have red noses and large ears, this enables them to smell things and hear things much better.

The clothing they wear is often made from wool which they find in the fields where the sheep have been. However, they can find other useful materials left by people. Possibly, they are called Thermalins because they do not like the cold and use the wool to wrap up well in the winter.

This story is about one family of Thermalins who lives in a village they call Muchwood in a wood near a human village called Hazeldown. There are houses being built nearer to the woods which at the moment are too far away to trouble the Thermalins. The family consists of Grobalin, the father, who sometimes is a bit grumpy, especially as he tends to be clumsy. However, he is good-hearted and loves his wife and children. Amelin, the mother, is very much in control of the family as she feels it is her job to keep them safe. She is loved by her family and everyone in the village, they all pop in to see her for help when needed. Bosalin, called Bosy by his friends, is the eldest child at twelve-years-old. Softalin, his sister, called Sofy is ten-years-old. The baby girl is called Beenalin, although shortened to Beeny, and she is only three-years-old. They all have friends in the village, although sometimes they have to play on their own when their friends' families go searching or to see relatives in other villages.

Chapter 2
The Children of Witchwood Close

Hazeldown is a small village in the country where recently, new houses have been built. Three new houses on the edge of the village are just two miles from the woods where the Thermalins live. The three houses that are in Witchwood Close were occupied recently by three young families.

The Lamberts have two children. Alex, who is five and Jessica, who is ten and they live in number two. In number four live the Newtons, who have three children. Sam, who is six, Rebecca, who is eight and Richard, who is twelve. The Reeds stay at number six and they have two children. Molly, who is ten and Lucy, who is eight.

Although the children have only lived in the close for three months they have already played together, as they moved in April and have been able to play together out in a safe area. Alex and Sam are the youngest and are often seen together with their tricycles. Rebecca and Lucy, both eight, have become good friends who enjoy writing and drawing. Richard, Jessica and Molly are also good friends and like playing games on their computers and active games outside. However, they often play together so they can all have fun.

The children are lucky in that they all attend the same school—Hazeldown Junior although Richard will soon be going to the high school in the big town, Framton.

One day when they were all called together in the schoolyard by Richard who said, "Why don't we form a club?"

They all agreed that it was a good idea. Molly suggested it could be called the Witchwood Friends which they became and even years later, they still meet up on special occasions.

Rebecca and Lucy set about designing a club badge and Richard managed to persuade his parents to use their summer house at the back of the garden as a clubhouse.

Chapter 3
Muchwood

In Muchwood, all the little houses are different, built by the older Thermalins when a young couple gets married and then extended as the family grows. The Thermalins only have one name each, therefore this family is called the Grobalins after the dad, who is the eldest in the household.

The house the family lives in is larger to fit them all in. The kitchen and dining room is a large open-plan, and the other room is big and cosy with an open fireplace for logs in the winter. From the kitchen, a staircase runs up to the four bedrooms and good-sized bathroom. The house has three doors: the back, front and roof, in case of fire.

The village consists of a little community of ten houses with both young and older Thermalins living in them. All have jobs to do that help the community to run smoothly. Grobalin makes shoes and boots in a workshop which he built beside his house. Bosy has a friend called Docalin or Doc, whose dad, Camalin makes butter and cheeses. Although old Tobylin should be retired, he still makes suits for the male Thermalins. Most of the mothers make their own clothing but they will help each other in times of difficulty.

They all have gardens and grow things from whatever seeds they can find; a lot of what they eat comes from the woods and the surrounding fields.

The houses form in a big circle, at the centre they have built a meeting hall and games room where they gather often in the evening. Some of them have made musical instruments from wood they have found, usually pipes and drums. They sing and dance to tunes passed on from their old relatives.

The children have many games that they play such as hide the acorn or throw the conker. There is no school as they learn from their parents and have to help with the household duties and the foraging for food.

In general, they have a happy life in the area they live in, which is very remote, they do keep an eye on the outside world where human houses are getting nearer.

Chapter 4
Family Outing

One early morning in the late summer when the sun was just coming out in a bright blue sky, Amelin was down in the kitchen of the little Thermalin house. The children, Bosy, Sofy and Beeny were eating their breakfast of berries and home-made flakes made from oats and barley seeds.

Grobalin had just woken up after hearing the noise downstairs. He came down the stairs half-asleep grumbling, "What's going on at this time in the morning? It's only six o'clock."

Unfortunately, he missed the last step and tumbled over a side table that had been left at the bottom, at that he shouted out, "Who the devil has left that in the way! Have the fairies been in here again?"

The other family members could not reply they were so busy laughing. He was not hurt, only his pride was hurt.

Amelin went to fuss over him saying, "I was just about to come up and get you up, are you all right?"

Grobalin said, "Of course I am!"

And they both set about laughing again.

At that he said, "Answer my question, what's

going on?"

Amelin explained that a fairy had arrived with a message from her sister, who lived in another village called Camton, in the great forest. Her sister had just had a baby and she just had to go to see her. Grobalin agreed that it was a good idea and that they should set off as soon as possible before the Elves were about. They often came into the forest about this time of year and could cause trouble.

So they packed all they needed for the journey, then asked the rabbits who lived nearby to carry them as they had trained them to help them. The distance they had to go was about ten miles, they passed the fields nearer to Witchwood Close and on passing a number of farms till they came to moorland.

On a high point, they stopped for a rest and to have a snack of water and cheese with bread and jam. Suddenly Bosy shouted out that he had seen some Elves in the distance, however, they were heading in the direction of another wood away from them.

"Good," said Grobalin, "that means they will not be stealing from our village."

By lunchtime they had reached their destination where they were greeted by Amelin's sister, Subalin and her husband, Michalin. They all gathered round the new baby called Snugalin, who was so very tiny.

A lunch was prepared of potatoes, carrots and wild herbs which was enjoyed by all. The young Thermalins played games outside so as to allow the baby to have a sleep and their parents to talk. After about an hour, it was time to return home to Muchwood. They said their goodbyes, packed up and mounted the rabbits for the trek home.

On their way over the moorland, Sofy said, "Is that smoke over toward the east?"

They all stopped to look and could see that a smoke cloud was getting larger.

Grobalin said, "It could be a farmer burning waste."

Suddenly rushing towards them, came two hares and six rabbits, all with Thermalins on board. On reaching them, they looked terrified.

The lead Thermalin stopped, greeted the family, and reported that their village had been set alight by a band of Elves who had stolen food and clothes while most of the villagers were out foraging. They had seen the Elves leaving towards the east and decided it would be better to head west to warn the families in Muchwood and build new houses where there were more Thermalins.

Grobalin said, "Why did the Elves burn your village? They were not usually so violent they were just greedy and helped themselves."

The senior Thermalin from the village called Downwood, said he had seen a Thrall with the Elvin band. The Thralls came from the far north and did not normally come down south, they were nasty and cruel, leading the Elves to plunder and burn.

"Right," said Grobalin, "you will be welcome in our village." To Bosy he said, "You must go back to Camton and warn them what has happened so they can be prepared if the Elves come their way. Be very careful and come back straight away before dark, good luck. The rest of you, mount up and follow me back to Muchwood."

When they got back a meeting was held, and the story told to all at Muchwood, an agreement was made to welcome the other Thermalins. They stayed in the other families' houses for a time. However, the next day they all helped to clear the woods to build new houses for the newcomers.

Another thing they should do was to have an early warning system in case the Thrall and Elves came their way. So it was agreed to ask the wood fairies to help.

Grobalin met the queen fairy in their glen, and she was only too willing to send some of her troops to the east to track the villains.

Chapter 5
The Witchwood Friends Meet the Thermalins

A meeting had been called by Richard for the friends to get to the clubhouse at the back of the Newtons' garden as soon as they could after tea. The children and their families had all been away on holiday and as they arrived, they were busy discussing their holiday adventures.

In the clubhouse it was cosy and set out with enough chairs for them all, with posters of their favourite pop and football stars on the walls.

Richard said that they only had two weeks left of the school holidays and they should plan some outings together. Molly was keen to go fishing in the lake beyond the big wood; Sam and Alex wanted to go to the park in the town, which meant a bus ride.

"All right," said Richard, who was the eldest, "we should think about it and come back here tomorrow night with ideas and vote on what we should do."

The next day, Sam and Alex asked Molly if she would come with them to play in the little stream over the fields nearer to the wood. The other children were out shopping. Sam, Alex and Molly got permission and off they headed into the field at the back of the houses. All around the fields were full of wheat or barley ready to be harvested. When they got to the stream, they took off their shoes and socks and waded in to set about building a dam which the boys loved to do.

Molly sat on the bank and made a drawing of the dam builders with the pencil and paper she had brought in her satchel; she was a very good artist for her age. After an hour or so the boys had made a really good paddling pool; so they waded in looking for water creatures and having a happy, splashy time. Eventually, it was time to head for home for tea and the evening meeting. So on the way back, they were talking about what they could do as an outing.

As they reached the first field leading home, a shortcut was to go through the centre of the field where the wheat was nearly as tall as Molly. So off they went carefully, so as not to damage the plants.

When they had reached about halfway, Sam said, "I can hear a funny, little noise, like a faint crying."

They all listened, and yes, it was coming from their right in the field. After searching for some time, they were amazed to find a very tiny person looking very frightened and lost. Who was this little child with a red nose and big ears?

Bosy had arrived back at Muchwood just as it was getting dark, he reported to his parents that the Thermalins at Camton were now preparing a watch to look out for the Elves gang.

He said that as he passed back over the moors,

he had seen the gang camped and was unsure which direction they were headed.

Grobalin said, "Don't worry, we have the fairies on the lookout as our early warning system in case they head this way."

Elves were about the same size as the Thermalins, with long, pointed ears and pointed noses, their hair was kept long and usually tied at the back. Most of them had blue or green hats. Unlike the Elves, the Thermalins kept their hair short and wore woolly, white hats in the cold weather. The Thralls, on the other hand, were at least three centimetres taller with small ears, big, flat noses, wide bodies and green hair. They are really ugly creatures. Like the Thermalins, they have the magic to make themselves invisible to humans.

The next morning, as most of the older Thermalins were busy building extra houses for the new arrivals, Bosy asked his friend, Doc to come with him to gather some seeds in the fields below the woods. Beeny, who was playing with her dolls heard this and pleaded with him to take her with them. So after asking Amelin if it was OK, they set off with strict instructions to look after the toddler, the baby of the family.

It should be noted that Thermalins under five-years-old are unable to use the magic to make themselves invisible, they relied on the older ones' magic.

It was a lovely summer's day as they set off for the fields. In the woods they passed a group of fairies who were making a tree house, they waved at them and said one of their brothers was off keeping an eye on the Elves.

In the fields they started collecting seeds that had ripened and after some time had nearly filled the basket that Bosy had brought.

Doc had found an old conker that he and Bosy started to use to play football which took their attention away from little Beeny. She had wandered deeper into the field following a field mouse, which now was running through a hedge into the next field, and still she followed until she realised, she had lost her way.

Both the boys and Beeny were shouting now, "Where are you?"

But neither could hear the other. It was getting late by the time Bosy and Doc decided they should go for help. At this time, Molly, Sam and Alex had found Beeny, who was too afraid of these big people she had not ever seen before that she did not speak.

Molly said, "We cannot leave her in the open on her own, crying."

So they all agreed to take her to the clubhouse on the way home and that they would say nothing to anyone until they had their meeting after tea with the other club members.

On reaching the clubhouse, they managed to find a big wooden box, a cushion was placed in it for Beeny. They found a toy cup and gave her some water and some cake they got from their houses.

Beeny was not so frightened now, as the children were very kind and looked after her. She had some water and cake then fell asleep. It was not long before Molly had finished her tea and returned to the clubhouse. As she waited for the others to come, she managed to get Beeny to tell her what had happened and who she was, a Thermalin.

All the children were completely amazed at the little person they had never seen the like before. Beeny, who was now feeling braver, told them about her village in the woods and they all agreed it was their duty to take her back. Jessica said they should make a promise not to tell anyone, not even their parents about the little people. They all agreed and set off with Beeny to take her home before it got dark.

It was now six o'clock in the evening. However, it did not get dark until after ten o'clock, so they would have time to get back home before their parents missed them. Molly sat Beeny on her little rucksack and off they tramped over the fields which took them a good hour, they entered the woods singing, 'I love to go a wandering'.

Suddenly, little Beeny shouted out, "Mammy and Daddy!" At that the children were shocked to see a crowd of little people had appeared, it seemed out of nowhere.

When Bosy and Doc had returned without Beeny, pandemonium had broken loose. Amelin and Grobalin were very upset; after a quick meeting with the whole village people, they all set out to find the lost toddler before it got dark.

Thus, it was that the two parties met, both surprised at the meeting.

Once Beeny had told the other Thermalins how the children had looked after her, Grobalin said, "We are very thankful for your help in looking after our Beeny, you could come to see our village provided it is kept a secret."

So they arranged for Bosy to meet the children at the same place in the morning at nine o'clock. Richard said they should all return home now as it was getting late. Grobalin agreed and at that point the Thermalins disappeared and were gone.

The children headed home. Lucy was the first to speak and said how wonderful it had been to meet the Thermalins. Rebecca said she could not wait to see the village. Richard reminded them all of their promise *never* to tell anyone. As they reached the clubhouse, they agreed to meet in the morning at eight o'clock with some food such as bread and cereal and drinks, further, to tell their parents they were going on a picnic in the woods to build a hideout. Beeny had told the children that some other Thermalins had just come to the village, so they were building new houses for them.

Most of the children's parents had to go to work, so the parents had come to an arrangement with Richard's mother, who worked from home. So the parents were glad the children had formed a club and could stay with the Newtons in the house or in the clubhouse.

It had been a long, hot summer which meant the children were always outside or in the clubhouse playing or doing activities together, so it was not unusual for them to be going out together. Mrs Newton always told the older ones, Richard, Molly and Rebecca, to look after the younger ones, particularly Sam and Alex who tended to get into trouble, such as falling into puddles, or more likely jumping into puddles.

Next morning, the children gathered at the clubhouse with their rucksacks full of sandwiches, drinks of orange or Coke in their cool bottles and whatever tools they could carry. Jessica and Alex had hammers and nails; Lucy and Molly had screwdrivers and pliers and a box of screws. Sam and Rebecca had saws of different sizes and Richard had a hand drill, a plane and two hammers.

Everyone was feeling excited to be going, the sky was blue, the morning air was clear, a beautiful day. Richard checked if everyone was ready. Unfortunately, little Sam still had his slippers on so Richard made him and Rebecca, who had sandals on, go and put more suitable shoes or boots on for a hike.

Five minutes later they were all ready and set off on the way to the fields.

Chapter 6
Off to the Woods

Crossing the fields, the children sang songs to entertain the younger ones and to take their minds off the long walk. One of the favourites was, 'The wheels on the bus go round and round'. On reaching the entrance to the woods they stopped at the arranged meeting place. However, no one was there so Richard checked his watch and remarked that they were only a minute late. Suddenly, there was Bosy made visible when they arrived.

Bosy said he was happy to see them and told them to follow him and be careful not to trip up on roots and stones they must walk over as they had to go deep in the woods. After at least three miles or so it seemed, he led them up a hillside, where many thick bushes were growing that seemed unlikely to get through. At a touch of his hand on a bush, a way opened up as if by magic and they passed through.

What a sight awaited them as they looked down on a circle of land, hilly on all sides, with a flat, level area at the bottom. Into the hillsides were little houses already built and in other places building work was going on. Grobalin and the other Thermalins greeted them and showed them what they were building. They were digging out of the hillside then making rough wooden frames which they fixed into the dug-out area and then covered them again with soil and grass turf. Some of the wooden joints were difficult to make as the Thermalins used rope or twine which were very well made but took a lot of time to make. When the children showed the Thermalins their tools and equipment they were overjoyed, then the children set about helping them to build the frames, screwing them together was much faster.

At lunchtime, they had almost finished the frames for the new houses which pleased the little people who brought out fruit and special scones they made to give them to eat. The children shared their food with the Thermalins, so they all had a good time over lunch.

After lunch it did not take them long to finish the frames and then start covering them with soil and turf, which they all joined in with. Sam and Alex loved this as they could slide down the hillside playing with the other young ones from the Thermalin village.

Time passed quickly as they were busy. However, they finished the outside of the houses by evening, the little people would be able to do the inside themselves.

Richard said they would return the next day, Grobalin said that they could return to visit them anytime without notice, that they were now friends of the Thermalins. So they packed up their goods and after farewells and goodbyes, Bosy and Sofy led them back onto the path to return home.

After a while Molly said, “I think we can find our own way to the fields we know the way now.”

Richard agreed, so they waved bye to Bosy and Sofy as they returned to Muchwood. On their return home, the children were really tired after the long day of walking and helping to build. They all went straight in to dinner with a promise to meet again in the morning to return to the little village.

Although all the children were rather dirty after the day’s activities, Sam and Alex were absolutely scruffy. So after telling their parents they had been sliding down the hillside, they were all told in each household to get a bath and into their pyjamas. Nothing more was said as they often ended up dirty.

The next day dawned fresh and bright after a rainy night. They all met at the clubhouse to decide the plan for the day. Jessica and Molly suggested they make a playground for the young Thermalins.

Richard, who always thought ahead said, “We must make our own shelter in case of bad weather as we can’t get into a little village house.”

Lucy piped up, “Everyone needs to wear strong boots or welly boots because of the night rain which will make the going wet.”

After packing all they needed for the day, they set off over the fields to the woods with Alex singing, ‘Once on a hill stood a lonely goatherd’, the others joining in the chorus. Once they had reached the wood, they followed the path they were on the day before, however after a mile or so they were not sure which direction to go in when the bushes got thicker. Fortunately, a returning fairy from the fairy watch saw them as she was heading for the village, made herself visible and guided them in.

Greetings were made to the Grobalins. Before they got back to finishing the houses, Richard asked if it was all right if they made a playground for the little ones; they were highly delighted with the idea, after that he told them about the plan to build their own shelter. It was agreed that it was a good suggestion, but Amelin said it would be better if they built it away from the village a little so as not to attract attention, it would be done. The fairy called Fussy, who had seen the children into the village had reported to Grobalin that the Elves, led by the nasty Thralls, were heading west but it would be a long time before they reached the woods.

The children set about building the playground. Sam and Alex who were very practical for their age, built a seesaw, they helped the little ones on and taught them to sing, seesaw madgery daw. Richard and Molly built a slide which went down very well to the delight of the children. Rebecca, Lucy and Jessica managed to build a climbing frame that was quite solid and safe for the little Thermalins. The little Thermalins happily scampered up, swinging like little monkeys. Everyone was thrilled to see the playground.

The children were led to a place by Bosy and Doc which was just outside the village where they could build their shelter or Den as the boys would call it. The ground was level, and a number of bushes were nearby. These had big leaves which they cut down and used to form a roof over a frame made after collecting wood from coppice bushes. They made the frame using vertical poles joined by horizontal poles, forming a shelter like a log cabin.

"Would you believe it?" said Molly.

on completing the Den, the heavens opened with heavy rain, they all rushed inside and found it quite comfortable, they had made a wooden bench seat and brought in some hay from the fields. A summer shower was soon over, however, it had proved how well the Den had been made as there was only one little leak which they soon repaired.

They said goodbye to Bosy and Doc who had

worked with them, thanked them for showing them where to find wood and hay and promised they would visit Muchwood again as soon as they could.

By this time, it was getting near dusk, the children got together all their tools and stuff, as Sam would say, then they packed their rucksacks. The trip back was easy now as they had got their bearings, so they could now find their way in the woods to the fields they needed to cross to get home. They arrived home without any more events, tired but happy and very hungry. Richard said they should meet up at the clubhouse in the morning, then realised it was Saturday then Sunday when most of them went out with their families, or to church, so they would meet on Monday.

Chapter 7
The Elvin Gang

Elves live in the north, usually deep in caves which are entered from the mountain sides. They build villages and sometimes cities where there is water within hidden valleys underground. Much further north in the highlands live the Thralls, who don't normally wander away from their homeland unless they want to pillage.

They are rarely seen in the Thermalin lands as far south as Muchwood. However, the Thrall called Drogan had come down looking for his brother, Mostin and had come across the Elvin gang as they were heading out to steal from the Thermalins. He persuaded the Elvin leader called Amble, to help him look for his brother as they headed south.

In the west and east there were Thermalin villages, further west and east near to the coasts lived the Changelins, who were cousins of the Thermalins. They too could make themselves invisible, the main difference between them was they could change their legs into flippers and swim like mermaids. This meant they could catch fish easily and made good fish and chips. Sometimes the Grobalin family went to see their distant relatives at a village on the coast called Seascape.

The Elvin gang had headed east after camping overnight on the moors below Camton, Drogan said his brother might have headed that way and in any case according to Amble, there was a Thermalin village ten miles in that direction.

Amble had not been very happy at the burning of Downwood. However, Drogan had insisted and had taken over the command of the gang threatening to beat up anyone who disobeyed him.

Off they trekked over the moor till they reached another large wood, by this time it was getting late. The Elves, who always grumbled about something, wanted to make camp for the night. Amble said they should find a stream then set up camp, before they entered the wood. This time Drogan agreed, and it was not long before they had found a freshwater stream and had their campfires going.

At this time one of the fairies from the troop, who had been watching the Elvin gang for Grobalin, had seen where they were camped, which was near to the wood, went to warn the fairies she knew who lived there. The wood fairies lived deeper into the wood not far from a Thermalin village called Eastside, so they were able to warn the little people about the Elvin gang. They were made aware of the trouble caused at Camton, so they decided to pack everything up and head for the coast, to return later when the gang had moved on.

Drogan was awake first and shouted out, "Get up you lazy toads before I throw you in the steam!"

At that they all got busy making a quick breakfast then packed their big carry bags, like rucksacks made of hard-wearing twine that grew underground and started off into the woods.

After about two hours' march, they came to the area that Amble knew was the way to enter the village.

Drogan said, "Be quiet and we will surprise them."

They all crept through the thick bushes at the top of a mound of earth when suddenly, the earth gave way beneath them. The Thermalins had left a trap. A hole had been dug out and filled with water – which by then was muddy – and covered it with a weak frame with grass turf on top.

The fairies who had been watching at a distance, could hardly stop laughing and had a delightful time watching the performance.

What a terrible noise had come from the hole as they scrambled about to get out, soaking wet and raging mad.

Drogan and Able, still wet, shouted, "Come on, we will get them for this," and headed into the village screaming, "burn them, burn them!"

To their great surprise, there was nothing left but the deserted houses. They were all mad cursing the Thermalins, when they had calmed down a bit, Drogan asked where the next village was. Amble said there were no other villages to the east until they hit the coast, so they should head west. That was their normal route each year. Drogan asked if there were Thermalins in the west. Amble said there was a village called Muchwood.

He said, "We will head there and sort them out."

To say they were scruffy was an understatement. They were filthy dirty and by now tired out, so they decided to clean themselves in the stream at the edge of the wood and rest before their journey west.

Drogan, the Thrall who was very mad from what had happened to them and ready to be angry with the Elves, was about to settle down for the night, when a figure appeared from the wood, it was Mostin. He had heard the noise and had come to investigate. Drogan was delighted to find his brother.

Chapter 8
The Battle of Muchwood

It was Monday morning, the children of Witchwood Close had arrived at the clubhouse as planned, to decide on their next activities. After this week they all had to return to school, the elder ones were looking forward to seeing their school friends again. However, Sam and Alex remarked that they were not so keen on returning because they had really enjoyed this summer holiday. The others agreed.

Richard said, “Right, then we should plan some good activities, starting today.”

Lucy said, “We should go to the lake at the moor bottom.” Molly and Jessica said, “Why not go to the farm and pick some strawberries?”

Rebecca said, “I think we should visit our little friends in the wood and take a picnic to share with Bosy and his friends.”

In the end, they all agreed to go to the Thermalin village and ask if the Grobalin children could come with them on their outings.

“Right,” said Richard, “pack whatever you can for the picnic and come back to the clubhouse as soon as you can.”

So off they went to their own homes to get their rucksacks packed and ask their parents if it was OK to go for a picnic. Within half an hour, they had all returned to the clubhouse with permission, their parents liked them to all go together. So Mrs Newton was happy to let them go, telling them to be back before five for dinner.

Over the fields they went feeling happy, singing songs as they headed toward the woods. The fields had been harvested so they could take an easier route.

The Thralls from the far north, Drogan and Mostin, his younger brother, were happy to see each other.

When asked by Drogan why he had gone off from home he said, "I just wanted to see what it was like in the south. However, I got homesick and was on my way back north."

"Well," said Drogan, "we were worried when you went off on your own, so our parents sent me to find you."

"What are you doing with these Elves?" said Mostin, "are we going home now?"

Drogan told Mostin his story about meeting up with the Elvin gang and had gone with them because they knew the area.

"I am now determined to get our own back on the Thermalins." Once the Elvin gang had rested, Drogan and Mostin, who joined them, had some breakfast, packed up and set off west. They would head over the moors towards Muchwood.

In the village of Muchwood, the Thermalins had just about finished building the new houses for their new arrivals, so all was well until another fairy, called Groffy, arrived with news that the Elvin gang were now headed for Muchwood.

Grobalin called a meeting in the centre hall and asked all the little people to attend. He told them the Elvin gang was heading their way.

"What shall we do?" he said, "I feel that after all our efforts we should stand our ground and fight if necessary."

Some of the villagers were not happy with this as they had never resorted to violence; the newcomers who had already been burned out were ready to fight to defend their new homes.

Grobalin said, "I think there are now enough of us to overcome the Elves."

So, in the end, after a lot of discussion, it was decided to put up some resistance.

Amelin said the females should stay with the children in the hall while the males got ready to defend the village. Bosy, Doc and some of their friends wanted to help, so Grobalin said they could help find logs that they could fashion into weapons.

A frenzy of activity continued into the night as they prepared for battle without any sight of the Elvin gang.

By nightfall, the Elvin gang had almost reached

the wood where they had camped for the night after the long tramp over the moors. At first light they were up, collected the wooden weapons they had made along the journey west, and set off at a march through the wood towards the village, ready to steal and plunder.

The wood fairies had warned the Thermalins of the approach of the Elvin gang, so the little people were ready in the bushes as the Elves got near to the village entry.

The Elvin gang reached the rise leading to the entry bushes. Once they had pushed through, they assembled ready to charge down toward the village hall.

Suddenly there was a loud cry of, "Down with the Elves!"

The Thermalins rushed out of the bushes attacking. A cry of shock went up from the Elvin gang, but they soon fought back fearlessly.

Grobalin was fighting mad, wielding a big club, knocking down Elves until he met with Drogan, who was bigger and stronger. Drogan was about to smash down on him when the two boys, Bosy and Doc managed to see what was happening and hit his legs from behind. The fight was not going well for the Thermalins, so they retreated down into the level area to regroup.

Richard and the other children walked steadily over the fields, not aware of the approach of the Elvin gang who had gone into the wood just before them.

On reaching the wood, the children were happily following the path they knew led to Muchwood, when the wood fairies appeared. The fairy queen was very alarmed and explained to the children that a battle with the Elvin gang was going on and the Thermalins were in trouble. A fairy had seen the children as she headed for home and alerted the queen. She said they should get some sticks and run to help them. The children were bigger than the gang members and could carry larger sticks as clubs.

The Elvin gang was rushing down towards the now battered Thermalins shouting, "We will burn you all!"

The children entered the village to the great surprise and horror of the gang.

On seeing these large beings heading towards them screaming, "Charge," they were terrified and dispersed in all directions out of the village never to be seen again in Muchwood.

The Elves headed towards their mountain caves. Amble said he was relieved to see the Thralls run away. Drogan and Mostin had such a shock they never stopped running for miles towards the far north, each vowing never to head south again.

Grobalin and the other Thermalins were over-joyed that the children of Witchwood had rescued them from defeat and although many were battered and bruised no one was seriously hurt.

So to celebrate their victory in saving their village, Amelin said they should bring out food and drink and have a party for lunch. The children said they would bring their packed lunches; their rucksacks had been left in a hurry outside the village before the attack. All the little people cheered the children giving them many grateful thanks.

What a party they had! The fairies were invited and thanked for all their help. They brought a special drink made out of nectar from the flowers which the children thought delicious.

They brought out tables and chairs, built a big fire and roasted potatoes they had found left by a farmer; some had made cakes with wheat flour and wild fruit. Sandwiches and other good things to eat were shared from the packed lunches.

Everyone had a very good meal, after which Grobalin said they would always remember this day, it would be called Rescue Day and a village holiday.

Festivities continued, until at last Richard said, "It's time for us to return home."

Grobalin said, "You are now our special friends and are welcome here anytime, we all love you."

Waving to each other as they went out of the little village the children went happily on their journey homewards.

What a day it had been! By the time they reached the clubhouse it was after five, so tired out, they agreed to meet up again in the morning. Richard reminded them to keep their activities a secret as they headed to their houses.

Tuesday dawned, a wet and windy day. As the children met in the clubhouse it was thunder and lightning, the rain pouring down. It was too bad to play outside.

Jessica said, "Let's make a decision about our activities for the rest of the week."

Molly said, "We should decide each morning in case the weather gets worse."

The others were happy with a decision each day.

Richard said, "Right, what shall we do tomorrow?" Rebecca and Lucy, who had suggested the lake at the moor bottom, said they had been told by a school friend that there was a bigger lake with fish in and rowing boats further to the west of the woods.

"Goody," said Sam and Alex, "can we go fishing?"

"That's a good idea," said Richard, "do you all agree?"

"Yes," they all piped up.

They got busy drawing and painting until lunchtime. Lunch was held at the Newtons' house, some had burgers and chips, others had sausage and chips and Molly had egg and chips.

After lunch, the weather had changed when they met up again in the clubhouse.

Molly said, "Oft a dark and cloudy morning turns out a bright, sunshiny day."

The boys were eager to go out.

Richard said, "It is too late to go far but someone should and ask the Thermalin children if they would like to go fishing."

Richard set off with Sam and Alex, as they were too young to go on their own, leaving the girls to prepare for the fishing and finish the drawing.

Off they tramped over the fields, into the woods and on to the little village, all the little folk were now visible to the children. On the way, they passed a group of fairies who were busy making a fairy house in an old tree, the fairies chattered in their tiny voices saying how happy they all had been to see the Elvin gang chased away.

On reaching Muchwood, they were made welcome, Grobalin was happy to let his children go with them in the morning and said he would see who wanted to go and make sure they were ready.

Chapter 9
The Western Lake

Wednesday was another bright and sunny day. The children met at the clubhouse with permission to go fishing; some had their fishing rods and others, their fishing nets, and jars. Rucksacks were packed with lunch meals and rain gear, just in case of rain later. They all had their welly boots on because the ground was wet, and they would be useful at the edge of the lake. It took about an hour to reach the little village; they knew their way well now and reached their destination without any mishaps.

On arrival, they were met with happy waves and greetings, Bosy, Doc, Sofy and several other Thermalin children were ready with their fishing tackle. They often went fishing in the streams and the moor lake, which was not very far, just outside the wood. Beeny was begging Grobalin to let her go as well, Amelin said she could go, but she made the children promise to look after the tiny ones.

Most of the little ones got a lift on the rucksacks as they all set off to the big lake. Bosy and Doc said they knew the way through the wood, so they headed west to find the lake. At the edge of the wood, they came out onto a narrow road which was leading further west; however, they could not see any sign of the lake. So Richard said he would climb a nearby tree to see over the hedge and into the distance.

At the top of the tree, Richard shouted down, "I can see the lake and there is a track leading to it around the next bend."

At that point they heard a clip-clop of horses' hooves. They moved aside to let two ladies riding along pass them. The ladies could not see the Thermalins and asked the children where they were going, they then directed them to a gate further to the right which was the quickest way to the lake. After going through the gate, a path led them past some fields to the lake which was surrounded by trees and quite deserted, except for the boating harbour nearby.

They all gathered around a quiet spot at the edge of the lake and got their fishing gear ready, some had brought worms and others maggots. Richard had a proper fishing rod, the other children had nets and lines. There were plenty of small fish which the young children were busy catching and putting in their jars. The fish were just the right size for the Thermalins to eat, a little small for the children. Richard caught some lovely rainbow trout. After fishing for a long time, some of the Thermalins caught some trout and other fish; they were not sure of the name of them.

By this time, it was lunchtime so they all settled down and had a much-needed break under a big oak tree at the lakeside.

It was then that Jessica said, "How many of you

have some money?"

Between them they counted £4.

"Good," said Jessica, "we can hire a boat and fish from it out on the lake."

"Yes," said Sam. "Can we do that?" he asked Richard.

"A good idea," said Richard, who was the eldest, "but finish your lunch first."

When lunch was finished, they packed up all their gear and went around the lake to see the boatman, he charged £1 for the boat and £1 per hour. They hired a boat, which was large enough to take them for two hours.

The boatman, of course, could not see the Thermalins. They clambered aboard and settled down getting ready their fishing gear as Richard who could row headed out into the centre of the lake. Once they had stopped, fishing began again. Molly caught a carp and Lucy managed to catch a roach, the others were catching young trout and catfish.

Richard had let Bosy, and Doc borrow his fishing rod, they caught a trout and were delighted, then cast off again. Suddenly, there was a great tug on the line which pulled the boys over the boat into the water. Fortunately, Richard was able to scoop them up with the rod, then he and Rebecca held onto the rod, as they pulled the line in, the others were all concerned at seeing the wet Thermalins.

As the line came in, they were all amazed at the size of the fish: it was a massive pike with a body that was four-foot long with big teeth. Three of them tried to pull in the pike but it was so strong that the boat was being pulled along at quite a speed.

They all had to hang on tight to the boat rails. The boat was heading towards the boathouse, they were terrified of crashing when the line snapped, and the fish was gone. Richard rowed to the landing stage to disembark, they all got out relieved to be out of the water after seeing the pike. As they gathered their gear to go Richard told the boatman what had happened.

The boatman said, “I saw what happened! Not many people get to see old Goliath, the big pike. He has been in the lake for years and none of the fishermen have been able to catch him. He is very smart.”

They said goodbye to the boatman, then, having decided it was time to go, they set off back to the little village in the wood. It did not take long to get back and on their arrival, the little Thermalins were eager to tell Grobalin and the others about their adventure.

Bosy said although they were a little frightened, they had good fun and had caught a lot of fish. The children shared the fish out leaving enough for the Thermalin families and the rest to take home to Witchwood.

Richard asked Grobalin if they could call in the morning to take the children with them again, depending on the weather, although they had not decided where they were going yet. As the little children pleaded with him.

He said, "Of course they can go, pick them up on your way, all being well."

That evening there was a smell of fish in the little village as the families cooked their evening meal.

Amelin told her children how nice the trout was, and they should go themselves to the Western lake.

Bosy said, "If we had caught that pike the whole village could have shared it."

Sofy and little Beeny agreed.

Grobalin said, "I wonder if I could catch it." They all had a good laugh at that.

The Witchwood children had set off homewards through the wood and across the fields, a way they knew well now and arrived back in time for their evening meal, possibly fish.

Richard said, "We should meet afterwards at the clubhouse."

Jessica said, "Make it seven o'clock because Alex

and Sam have to be in by eight o'clock."

Off they went to their own houses feeling rather tired after an exciting day.

Molly was first to arrive at the clubhouse followed shortly by the rest of the children. They settled down to have a meeting after Richard had stopped the chattering.

"Can we now decide what we will do tomorrow and Friday?" said Richard.

"Yes," said Molly, "remember we are back at school on Monday so it's the end of our holidays."

"Right," said Rebecca, "I have been told it's good up at the caves that are at the top of the moorland, what do you think?"

Lucy said, "It's a long way, about six miles."

Jessica said "We would have to set off early to make sure we get back in time."

Alex and Sam said, "Come on it will be super fun, we can climb on the rocks and play hide and seek."

"Very good," said Richard, "we meet at eight o'clock in the morning, remember to bring your lunch. What about Friday in case we are late back?"

"A treasure hunt," said Lucy, "we could set off from the little village."

"All right," said Richard, "I will plan a route and layout clues for you all to find the treasure I will bury."

"Shall we go and play on our bikes now?" said Sam to Alex. "See you in the morning," they all said in chorus.

Chapter 10
High Ground

It turned out another lovely day and by now Mrs Newton was used to the children going out on their adventures as Sam and Alex called their activities. So she made packed lunches for the children and reminded Richard to be firm with the younger ones and look after them. At the clubhouse, they all gathered with their rucksacks around eight as agreed. Richard checked that they all had good shoes or boots on and off they went over the fields and into the wood.

On the way through the woods, they were seen by the fairies who were now living in a big tree near the path to the village. Jessica told them they were heading for the high ground. Groffy and Fussy, the two fairies who lived in the tree said they would like to go with them. So off they all went to the village where the Grobalins were waiting with a group of Thermalin children.

They all had their tiny bags like rucksacks but made with special twine in which they had their packed lunches, they said farewell to Grobalin Amelin and the others and set off up north through the woods.

What a sight they were, if they could be seen!

Seven children, two fairies and ten little Thermalins who were being carried by the children all chatting away merrily as they walked.

Once they left the woods and went on to the moors, the ground started to go uphill steadily until they reached rockier outcrops and then lots of boulders at the top. What a view they had, in the distance was the woods, the lake and even Hazeldown. Far into the distance, they could just see the mountains and the great forest.

Richard declared he was ready for lunch so after their long walk they were all hungry, they found a big flat rock they could all sit on and had a really happy time having a picnic, sharing some food and drink. The fairies and the Thermalins thought it was a great treat.

After lunch, they packed their remains away and left them on the flat rock and went climbing on the rocks that were easy to climb, one of the rocks that somehow had ended up sloping down they used as a slide. What fun they had.

Sam called out, "Shall we play hide-and-seek now?"

"Right," said Molly, "I will be one team leader and Richard the other."

Two teams were selected: one team to hide, the other to search and bring the captives back to the flat rock. Richard's team scattered to hide while Molly's team waited and counted to twenty, then set off to find them. After some time, they managed to find all of Richard's team and were ready to swop.

Little Beeny said, "Where is my sister, Sofy?" They searched everywhere for Sofy then Lucy shouted out, "I heard a whimper down this little hole."

They all gathered around and could hear the faint noise, unfortunately, Sofy was very small and had tripped and fell down the hole.

Fussy said, "I can fly down there and see how she is."

So down she went to reappear to say, "Sofy is OK, just a little bruised but she is too heavy for me. However, I can see light at the other side of a cavern so I will go and investigate and let you know where the entry is to get in to her."

Soon Fussy and Groffy, who had gone with her appeared over the hilltop and led the others to an opening well-hidden between two rocks. They went down a narrow passage that suddenly broke out into a massive cavern which had just enough light for them to see. It was covered with stalactites and stalagmites formed by deposits of crystalline calcium carbonate on the rocks.

They found Sofy, who was very frightened and crying until she could see the others had arrived, she had been very lucky not to fall on a sharp rock, but on sandy soil. Richard picked her up in his arms to carry her out.

Rebecca shouted from further down the cavern

where she had been looking at the glowing rocks, "I can hear water."

They all stopped to listen then suddenly a stream of water started to run down the cavern.

Lucy said, "It must have been raining outside while we have been in here."

Fussy flew ahead and was soon back to say it was pouring down, it was then that Richard pointed to the stream that was running quicker and deeper all the time.

He said, "Come on everyone, we must get out of here in case it floods."

They all headed to the passage and up to the entry where they waited a while until the downpour stopped. It had been a summer cloudburst followed by bright sunshine, when they reached the flat rock, they found it had soaked their rucksacks. However, they were waterproof, so they got them on their backs ready to head home as it was late afternoon. It had been an exciting day and they had a long trek home.

Sofy was fine now bouncing about on Sam's and then Alex's shoulders. They were sorry Sofy had been hurt but as Bosy pointed out, without that having happened, they may never have found the cavern.

The party of little travellers had just left the rocky outcrops When Jessica, who had very good eyesight, looked up to the sky and said, "Look up there at that big bird."

The others had not seen it. However, as they

looked up it was getting nearer.

It was then that Molly said, "It's a golden eagle but a massive one that could carry away a sheep."

Fussy said, "We had better be careful, I have heard about an eagle that could carry off a Thermalin."

It was then that another massive one appeared. Richard, as usual, was the first to react, he shouted at the other children to collect some heavy sticks to use as clubs if required. Molly said, "Quickly, if we pile all our rucksacks together, we can hide the little Thermalins."

They were just in time as the first great eagle came swooping down. Fortunately, it worked, the eagle could not see the Thermalins, only seven brave children shouting and waving their clubs. The eagle just missed Sam as it turned upwards, who with great courage managed to hit the eagle's legs. That was enough for the eagles to return to the sky.

Soon they were out of sight.

"Good," said Richard, "let's head for the woods as quick as we can before they come back."

The children put the Thermalins in their rucksacks and at top speed, they soon reached the woods, with the fairies leading the way. The path to the little village was found and after a short walk, they arrived back safe and sound.

All the Thermalins gathered around to welcome them back. After greetings Richard said, "We had an exciting day today, but tomorrow is the last day of our holidays and we plan to have a treasure hunt, is it all right for us to call again in the morning?"

"Sure, it is," said Grobalin.

The children all said, "Goodbye and see you in the morning," and set off home.

What a story the little Thermalins had to tell, all about their adventures on the high ground as they all headed to their little houses for their evening meal. Amelin was concerned to hear about Sofy.

"I am all right, really," she replied, "but if it wasn't for that we may never have found the cavern."

Bosy said, "It was wonderful in the cavern."

Grobalin said, "I have never seen a cavern; maybe we could build one."

At that they all laughed.

Beeny said, "Daddy you could not build a cavern, it was made of rocks."

By the time the children reached Hazeldown, it was getting late, so they agreed to meet up in the morning at the clubhouse at nine o'clock.

Chapter 11
Treasure Hunt

Friday turned out a sunny day after a night of rain which was drying very quickly, making the gardens and fields smell lovely. Added to that, Mr Newton, who was off work on a Friday, was burning some old wood and furniture at the back of his garden.

"That is a gorgeous smell," said Molly to Lucy as they reached the clubhouse first.

"Yes," she replied, "I love the smell of burning wood."

Soon Alex and Sam arrived, followed by Rebecca and then Jessica, who looked around saying, "Where is Richard?"

"He left a message," said Rebecca, who is Richard's sister. "He has gone to the woods very early ahead of the rest of us to lay some clues for us to follow, the message said we should take packed lunches as before and he would meet us at the Den in the woods at about twelve o'clock."

"Right," said Jessica, "we had better get our rucksacks and lunch packs, we'll meet back here in fifteen minutes."

They were soon back, ready to go. They set off

through the back of the garden passing Mr Newton, who asked where Richard was. They told him why he had gone ahead. He wished them well telling them to be careful and not to be late back. After passing through the first fields into the one nearest the wood, they were surprised to hear familiar little voices. When they looked down, there was Bosy and Sofy with a group of Thermalins gathering seeds from the ground where the corn had been cut.

"Hello," said Molly, "we are off to the treasure hunt. Are you coming with us?"

"Yes," said Bosy, "but we promised to get some seeds before we go."

"We'll help," said Lucy.

So they all helped fill the Thermalins' sacks and even collected some extra in their rucksack pockets. Then they all trooped into the wood, a little later than they expected. They were heading for the little village, which they soon reached where they handed over the seeds to Grobalin. He was delighted to see so much, he got them to pour them into a large basket which he said would be distributed to the other Thermalins later.

The younger Thermalins, who were going on the treasure hunt, had gathered around the children. So they said farewell to Grobalin, and the party of treasure hunters went out of the village to where the Den was hidden away from the entry to the village.

Richard, who had been waiting, was a bit

concerned as it was well after twelve o'clock, he understood why after an explanation from Molly. It was time for lunch so they all sat in the Den and enjoyed their lunch while Richard told them how the treasure hunt would be run.

"I have tied a red ribbon around a number of bushes, trees and fences and left a written clue when you need to change direction. You will split into two groups as there are two ways to find the treasure. I have brought two spades, one for each group so you can dig up the treasure. When you find the treasure you must return with it to the Den. Good luck."

They all thanked Richard, then each group set off to follow their trail, one group headed west the other, north through the woods. Richard could only follow one group, so he opted to follow behind the western group. Molly was leading them with Alex, Sam, Bosy and Doc in her group.

The northern group was led by Jessica with Rebecca, Lucy, Sofy and little Beeny who was being carried by Jessica.

The starting point was easy as Richard told them which trail to take, the western group found the first red ribbon with a note saying, 'Look for a big tree that was used to build sailing ships.'

Molly said, "Does anyone know what he means?"

Sam was quick to answer saying, "It was the oak of England."

"Yes," said Molly, "we need to find an oak tree."

They found the tree after some searching, with another ribbon and note, this time it said, 'You must go up to leave the wood'.

They were a little puzzled about this until Bosy said, "Maybe we have to climb up somewhere."

Then Doc piped up, "I know a wall at the edge of the wood."

Doc led them to the wall but there was no ribbon in sight. Alex said, "Come on, I can see some wooden poles further down."

When they reached the poles, there was a double ladder that was used to climb over the wall with a red ribbon and another note tied to it. The note said, 'Clip-clop to this spot where you can drink your fill'.

Molly was the first to say, "It's a horse trough, come on, there's a farm in the distance."

Down the road they plodded and sure enough, they found another ribbon with a note attached to a hole at the top of the trough. This note said, 'Turn east where tractors plough and you will find a bushy brow'.

"Well," said Molly, "that path past the farm is heading east, let's go."

So they headed down the path looking for a ploughed field. After a while, Alex shouted, "I can see a field that's been ploughed."

They went in through a gate and started walking around the perimeter, at the bottom of the field they could see the ground was higher.

Bosy said, “That must be the brow with bushes behind.” When they got to the bushes, a red ribbon had a note attached to a bush which said, ‘Well done, dig for treasure’. Beneath the bush the ground looked disturbed, it was there they started to dig and soon discovered a biscuit tin full of a variety of biscuits and toffees.

“Hooray,” they all shouted. At that point, Richard appeared, he had been watching at a distance.

“Well done,” he said, “have a toffee each then we’ll take the rest back and meet the other group at the Den.”

Off they went and soon arrived back at the Den. The other group was not back yet so they sat and rested for a while when suddenly the two fairies, Groffy and Fussy who had seen the second group passing appeared at the Den.

Fussy said, “We joined the group and followed the clues, then we found the biscuit tin and the treasure, but the shovel broke so we are having a job to dig it up, so Jessica asked us to fly back and ask Richard to come with a shovel.”

“What treasure?” said Richard. “I only buried a tin, come on, let’s go and see what they have found.”

There was some excitement as they all headed north to find the others. It did not take long to get there with the fairies to guide them.

The others were waiting over the hole they had made to find the biscuit tin, but as Jessica pointed out they had broken the shovel when Lucy had tried to dig out a wooden box further down. Richard started to dig down carefully around at what was revealed as a wooden chest, they lifted it out with an effort to see it was well worn and decayed.

Richard prised it open to find it was full of gold coins. A gasp of shock came from them all as they saw the shiny treasure. At first, they thought it was the Queen's head on the coins, then Rebecca who had been looking at coins at school was sure it was Queen Victoria.

"Fill in the hole," said Richard, "we had better head back to the Den."

They did that, with the two boys on one side of the chest and Richard on the other they made it back. A big discussion took place, they decided to let the

Thermalins have one tin to take back to their village and they would take the other tin and the coins back to the clubhouse, then ask Mr Newton what they should do with the coins. What a day!

"What had been treasure hunt for biscuits and toffees turned out to be real treasure," said Lucy as they managed to get back to the clubhouse with the heavy chest.

Mr Newton was just getting ready to go in after being busy in the garden when he saw the children come back and wondered what they were carrying.

"Hello," shouted Richard, "come and see what we dug up Dad."

The chest had been placed open on the clubhouse table as Mr Newton went in to see what they had found and what a surprise he had at seeing the gold coins. They told him how they had found the coins as he inspected them.

Rebecca said, "We thought they may be Victorian," he gasped as he turned a coin over, there at the bottom was a date: 1704.

"Goodness!" he said, "they are not Victorian but from the reign of Queen Anne and very valuable. What we need to do after dinner is find out who the field belongs to where you found them, it is necessary in these cases for the finder and the landowner to share a reward."

After dinner, the three families of Witchwood Close gathered at the Newtons' place to see the coins, after which Richard and his dad got in their car to find the field where the coins were found.

They found the country track that led them to the field, where further along was a farmhouse. It was the farmers own land; he was called Mr Hopgood and on hearing the story he was delighted and said he had ploughed that field so many times and found nothing. They should inform the appropriate authority as it was a treasure trove.

Early the next morning, Richard and Rebecca went to the Thermalin village to see the Grobalin family. Richard had saved one of the coins and presented it to the family knowing that money was of no use to them. Grobalin was very pleased to receive it, he had heard the story of the find from his children but had not expected to get one of the coins.

Amelin said, "We will treasure it."

They all laughed at that.

"I will put it on the wall in the room," said Amelin.

It was like a picture to them. Little Beeny said the biscuits and toffees were scrumptious, on that they all agreed. The children said their goodbyes and they would visit again when they could, then off they went back to Hazeldown.

On Saturday and Sunday, the children went out with their families, this Saturday they were off to the big town Framton to get things for school.

Chapter 12
As Time Goes by

After many meetings with Mr Newton, Mr Hopgood and the local finds officer, the case of the coins came up at the Treasure Valuation Committee. The coins were very valuable and went to the British Museum, an award was given to be shared equally between the landowner and the finder of the treasure.

When the Newtons received the money, Richard said, "It is only right to share it between the three families as they were all been involved in the treasure hunt."

The money the children were given was put in bank accounts for them until they were eighteen, this would be very helpful when they went to college or university.

The children met in the clubhouse on Sunday afternoon, it was Molly who suggested they should take a gift to the Thermalins. They all agreed but what could they take that could be of use to them.

"I know," said Jessica, "seeds."

So they all said they would meet on Monday after school with seeds.

On the way from school, some of the children bought some seeds from the market while others got them from the local garden centre. On arriving at the clubhouse, they had seeds of every type, vegetables, fruits and flowers. Off they headed to the little village.

In the village the Grobalin family had been showing their friends the beautiful 'gold plate', as they called it, they were surprised to see the children arrive. Bosy, Sofy and Beeny dashed out to greet them followed by their parents.

"Hello," said Grobalin, "we didn't expect to see you so soon."

"Well," said Richard, "we have brought you a gift of seeds so you can grow some things you have never had before. They were overcome with thanks.

Grobalin said, "I will share them with all the Thermalins."

Now the children were back at school, the activities or adventures as Sam and Alex would call them had come to an end, especially as the bad weather was upon them. However, they still managed to get up to the Den and see the Thermalins when they could.

The following year, the Thermalins had lots of food and flowers from the seeds they had planted. From their plants, they were able to collect more seeds so they could continue growing year after year.

As the years went by, they had other adventures until a time came when the children had grown up and left home for college, university and some, the armed forces. Once they were sixteen, they could no longer see any of their little friends in the woods. No one else ever knew about the Thermalins, *until now*.

The Thermalins and the fairies still live in the woods, but they are difficult to find and can only be seen by good children.